Voglio una mamma-robot © edizioni ARKA, Milano, 2007
First published in this edition by Tundra Books, Toronto, 2008

English translation copyright © 2008 Marcel Danesi
Cover and interior illustrations reproduced with permission of edizioni ARKA

Published in Canada by Tundra Books,
75 Sherbourne Street, Toronto, Ontario M5A 2P9

Published in the United States by Tundra Books of Northern New York,
P.O. Box 1030, Plattsburgh, New York 12901

Library of Congress Control Number: 2007904174

Library and Archives Canada Cataloguing in Publication

Calì, Davide, 1972-
Mama robot / Davide Calì ; illustrations by AnnaLaura Cantone ; translation
by Marcel Danesi.

Translation of: Voglio una mamma-robot.
For ages 4-7.
ISBN 978-0-88776-873-6

I. Cantone, AnnaLaura II. Danesi, Marcel, 1946- III. Title.

PZ7.C1283Ma 2008 j853'.92   C2007-903759-3

We acknowledge the financial support of the Government of Canada through the Book Publishing Industry Development Program and that of the Government of Ontario through the Ontario Media Development Corporation's Ontario Book Initiative. We further acknowledge the support of the Canada Council for the Arts and the Ontario Arts Council for our publishing program.

ONTARIO ARTS COUNCIL
CONSEIL DES ARTS DE L'ONTARIO

Printed and bound in Italy

1 2 3 4 5 6 13 12 11 10 09 08

My mom is always busy.
She's at her desk every day,
sometimes even on Saturday.

When I get home from school, dinner's on the table
and there's a note that always says the same thing:

"I'm working. Brush your teeth after
you eat. Do your homework. Tidy up
your room. Hugs and kisses, Mom."

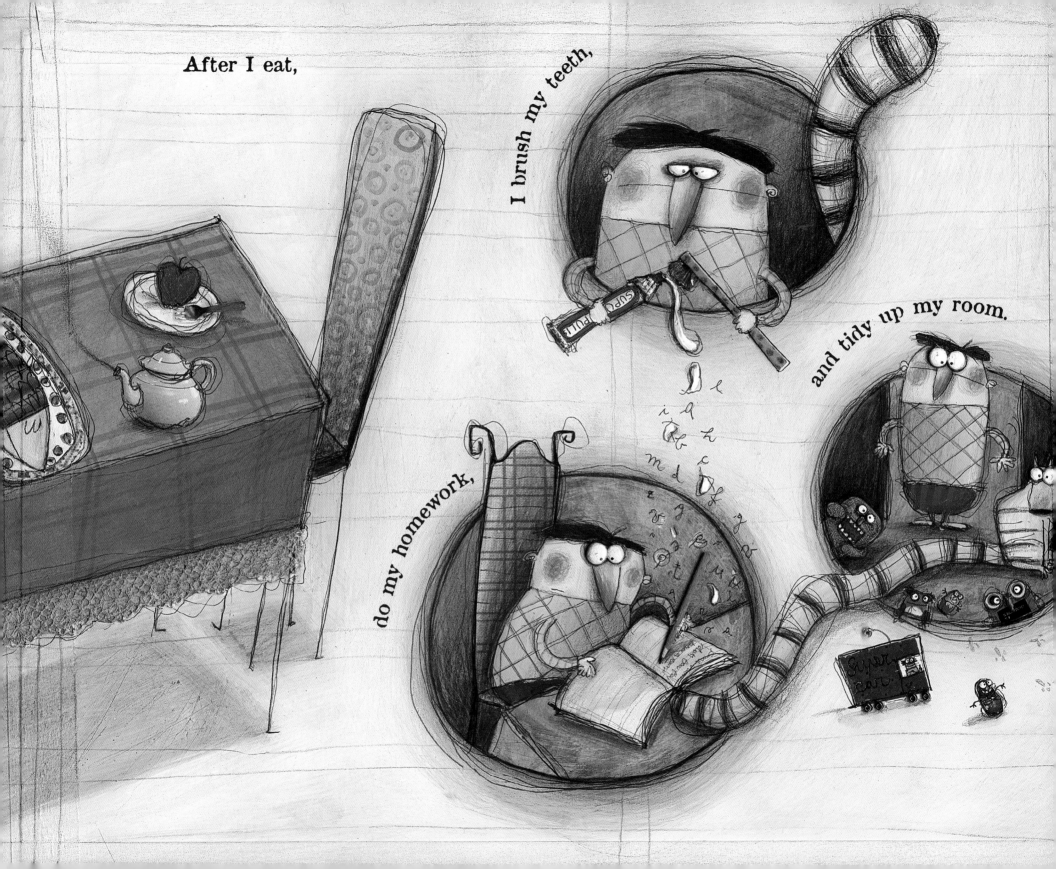

After I eat,

I brush my teeth,

and tidy up my room.

do my homework,

Then I play with my cat, Fluffy, and
pretend that he's a dog.

Boring. Boring. Boring.
Then one day, I have an idea.

I'll make a robot mom! Mama Robot would never be at
her desk. She'd spend all her time with me. She'd always
take me to school. I'd be the only one who has
a real robot for a mom.

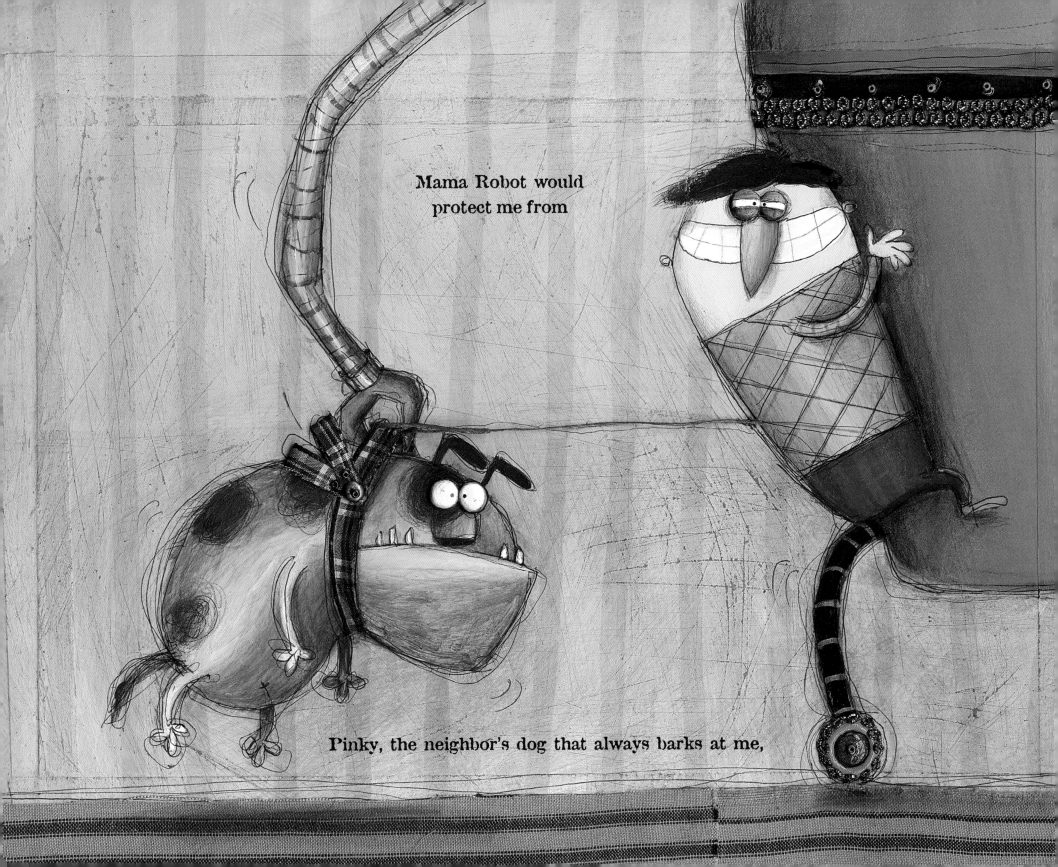

Mama Robot would
protect me from

Pinky, the neighbor's dog that always barks at me,

the bully at school that takes my morning snack,

the cars that don't stop at the traffic lights. . . .

and Mrs. Celestino from the third floor, who pinches my cheeks and calls me a "sweet little boy" whenever I see her in the elevator.

French fries, pizza,
popcorn, chicken nuggets
(like the ones on TV),
and, of course . . .
S P A G H E T T I !

She would NEVER make
boiled cabbage,
boiled fish,
boiled chicken,

boiled potatoes,
boiled vegetable soup, or
boiled peas.

Mama Robot would do all my homework for me.

Mama Robot would never be too busy to
SPEND TIME WITH ME!

She would never make me brush my teeth.

She'd let me stay up late
to watch scary movies

and would never make me
tidy up my room.

And best of all . . .

she would NEVER yell at me!

If she yelled at me, I would
TURN HER OFF
with my remote control.

Finally, my robot mom is ready.   There's only one problem.

HOW DO YOU HUG
A ROBOT MOM?

My robot mom isn't soft like my real mom.
My robot mom doesn't smell nice like my real mom.

My robot mom doesn't know how
to cuddle me like my real mom.

I've decided to take her apart
and build something else.

When Mom's finished her work, she gives me a big **HUG AND KISS.**

"WHAT'S THAT?" she asks.

"It's my robot dog!"